PANDEMITARY

By

Ed Chandler

Introduction

Written across the Pandemic, this series of thoughts and poems is just a confabulatory of words, a collection of the poet in my heart, my mind as it wonders lonely as cloud in a midst the storm.

As dawn broke and I awoke upon each new day of this epic ride we all call life I tried to compose a line, think a rhyme and without any crimes committed I eventually had this book...

Take a seat, take a drink, never take a human life and relax...

Words are words we all use them to love and to hate, please try to make sure you do the latter more, thank you.

All the best and to those of us that made it, well done, I think...

Contents

Lockdown

At first we all
Were afraid,
We waited to see,
Just how deadly
This virus would be...

As the lockdown started
As the pubs closed,
No place to buy clothes
And many shops
All shut,
No hair cut or gym,
Just the essentials,
The one form of exercise
And that was it
Into
LOCKDOWN!

Run

If ever you need,
The freedom of speed,
If you want to
Just get away...
Then RUN...

Run right now,
Just go out the door,
Take a book
Never look back
And just
RUN...

Time and again,
I'll be your friend,
On that or this
You can depend,
But if I fail
Then RUN,
Just RUN,
RUN for me,
RUN for you,
RUN for LifE...

LifE

Life Is A Two Letter Word...
If I had a penny,
For all my poems...
If I had a moment,
To say these words...
If I woke up...
If I got dressed...
If I confessed to a sin...
If I took my time...
If I saw you,
And you saw me...
If I help,
If I stand by...
If I live or
If I die...
If I cry at home...
If I eat an animal...
If I drink the wine,
If I have the reason...
If I have the power...
To me it's all about
IF...
For that's what LifE is,
If you do this,
If you do that...
If you do anything,
Just live...

Depart

I had rain in my heart,
I wanted to depart,
From this world,
From this time
And from this place...
But to me the concept
Of heaven or Hell,
Is all but a story,
One I did not tell...
Nor one I believe,
For to conceive
Such a thing
Would be unwise...
I'd rather face the truth,
When I depart
And let me heart stop,
My mind cease...
The last breath, the last word
The last moment
To be joy
To know that I am gone
Nothing more,
Nothing less...
For this I confess
Would be better
Than all the religion
All the false and blind faith,
To trust in a God,
That's just a
Human Invention!
I'd rather simply
Depart
And that be it...

Eleven

Just past the eleventh hour...
Sat halfway up a hill
Steep might the climb be,
But none the less, I go on...
To see the view, to look out
Upon the world
A piece of land, a whole species,
People pass me by
They think not of me or why...
They just go on, a bit like time
And this rhyme onto the Eleventh line...

~~~~~~~~~~~~~~~~~~~~

LWT

A lonely person,
Just the noise of the traffic,
An occasional bird call,
A dogs named yelled out...
No smack upon willow,
Of cricket ball...
A horse neighs
And all is calm,
Even the pig upon the tree
Doesn't grunt!
It's a stuffed toy,
Like the bear
Zebra and Chimpanzee!
They all sit quiet
Besides the
Lincoln Wish Tree
~~~~~~~~~~~~~~~~~~~~

Torn

When someone has hurt you,
And torn you apart...
If they take
A piece of your heart...

If love is gone...
If you are lost,
If you are lonely,
Torn and tattered...

Don't be battered
By the storm,
Come into the warm
Get out the way,
Take the day
And make way
For the sun,
For it will shine...
Shine in your heart,
So the tear will heal...

Love Me

Should I be unwise to,
Open up your eyes
To love me?

Is this love that I feel?
Is my dream real?
Will you take me now?
Will you let it be like,
They said it would be
Me loving you,
And you
Loving me?

Should I be unwise to,
Open up your eyes,
To love me?

Love me for me
Love for all
That we have
All that we need
Is love...

So won't you love me?
Come by my side
Hold me now and
Let us embrace
And love me
For I love you...

Come To Me

Come to me
Whenever you're lonely.
Come to me
If you need a shoulder
If you need a friend
On which to depend
Come to me...

Now and then,
You need someone older,
Someone wise,
Someone brave, so
Come to me
Just hide your fear,
Don't shed a tear...

Come to me
Whenever you're lonely.
Come to me
If you need a shoulder
If you need love
When you're alone
Come to me
For now and then,
If you need someone older,
If you want advice,
If you want freedom,
Then my friend...
Come to me

Cold

When you're out in the cold,
No one beside you,
And no one to hold,
When you've got
Nothing to lose,
Nothing to pay for,
Nothing to choose,
Nothing but hope
Nothing but fear,
No single tear
No words to say
Or time to play...

The cold will hold you
Take you in,
So don't begin
Try not to let it win,
For the cold
Is here...

~~~~~~~~~~~~~~~~~

20/02/2022

The palindrome,
The TWO of Tuesday,
We still wait
We still live
In this mad old world
But life goes on
So smile...
~~~~~~~~~~~~~~~~~

Empty

No toilet rolls
Or cigarettes,
Booze or beer,
Nothing to eat
No food for me,
No tins of this
Or tins of that
The rice has gone
And so has the pasta,
All that's left
A mouldy old plaster?
Empty streets,
Empty pubs
Empty gyms
Empty shelves...
Empty heads
And Empty hearts...
All as one
All in need
But too much speed,
Not enough thought...

Film

We all saw the light,
A flicker on the screen,
We awoke as if in a dream...
The nightmare of day
And the bleak of night...
A film of life
For it was real,
A Matrix
Or Twenty Eight Days Later,
In the midst of
Cruel Intentions
This V for Vendetta,
The life of Brian,
And more...
We fell into this film
We called it Covid or
Coronavirus,
Amongst other things...
It was the reality
Of a foolish nation
A complication owed to a bat?
No matter what
No matter why,
We all live
And
We all die...
So live your life
And enjoy the film...

Ramble

If we quit production,
Stop this world and
Turn me over,
Turn me now...
Simple things,
For nothing lasts forever...
Only lost now,
The moment is over...
A ramble of words
A lost moment..
A forgiven passion
A lover's lament
All time spent
Wasting a day away...

Fools...

It's a fool's game this,
Nothing but a fool's game
Standing in the line,
Waiting for the cure
And as we all
Feel like a clown
And try to turn
Our hidden frown
The right way up to smile,
No one will see if the mask
Hides it all
Are we just fools then?
To blind to see the misery
Of humanity...

To Words

To one lost,
To one to come,
To one gone
To this and the next,
To something over nothing,
To now and never
To the day
To the night
To when we meet
To the situation
To dreams
To all that and this
To a boy
To a man
To anything
To imagination
To lost items
To ask
To borrow
To lend
To send
To be
To see
To you and me...
To lavender
To the feel of sand beneath my feet
To one word
To the next,
To the poem
To the author
To WORDS...

Out

Not going out,
Not staying in,
Not being told
Not knowing who...
From all the news
The same old story
More dead
More loss
More or less
More rules
And nothing but a fool...
When we get out,
If we make it
To the next day
Then let us not rejoice
To a god
But to ourselves,
For we did this!
We humans
We one and all,
Forget the colour,
Gender or wealth
Forgive the believers and
Take the church out.
For we had no god
No time or money
No help form it
We did it alone
We got out
Out of food,
Out of suffering
Out of money
Out of hope
Out of our minds...

Noise

The call of an owl
Bark of a dog
The tree bark peals away,
And night turns to day...
Silence is golden,
So they say...
Who are they?
What do they want?
Why so much noise?
In a world of hate,
In a time of passion,
We all need a friend
We all need a drink...
Take back the night and
Hold onto the day
Make some noise
Make it loud and
Cheer for the end
The day to come
Not the day that passed...

Peace

On a bench
By a pond
At peace for now...
The willow tree,
A wish tree,
A ribbon in the wind...
I see all the woods
And nature of the world,
The calm
The peace of this place...

~~~~~~~~~~~~~~~~~~~~

Mask

On the train,
But I'd rather be on a plane...
Flying high
In the sky,
Off to Jakarta
And see my bebe...
I'll pass my house
Wearing my mask...
For we who are masked,
Pass the trees and fields,
The outside world has changed,
The sheep's and cows
Care not of Covid,
Nor do the birds that fly by...
As we pass lakes and rivers
We wait to take
Off the mask
And breathe again...
~~~~~~~~~~~~~~~~~~~~

Emotion...

Do you smile?
Do you frown?
Are you funny,
Like a clown?
Are you young or old?
Is that a moustache, madam?
You're emotion is lost
Hidden by the fabric
The plastic
The face covering...
Some wear the clear visor,
Like a broken helmet,
Walking and talking
Without emotion
We enter a bank
Wearing a mask,
But it's all normal now...
It's just what we do,
As we stand apart,
Two meters please...
I don't smell,
I don't bite, but the virus
The world just might!
So keep your emotion
Save the hand lotion,
For you'll need it later on...

Travel

But down your bag
Forget the holiday!
No one can go
To Dijon or Berlin,
Indonesia or Peru!
The Parliaments
The politicians,
The press and the pandemic...
The hysteric
The hype, the fear of a tissue...
Travel in your local area,
Nowhere else!
Don't travel for work,
If you can work at home,
Don't go see family or friends,
Just have a bubble,
That's all!
The long and the short, but not the tall!
Travel pass
And Covid checks,
Lateral Flow and PHQ tests,
Be sure you check,
Not once but thrice!
If you go out,
Only do so for a reason,
To exercise once,
To do an essential shop,
To get medicine,
That's about it...
So stay home
Be safe
And take care not to
Travel...

Mumble

Talking rubbish
We make no sense
In a riddle
Lost in translation
Talking about pop music
Only in a world
Of no tomorrow,
Do you see
The way to go home?

Do you mumble at me?
Do you see the light,
At the end of the tunnel?

Do you live or
Do you die?
Do you just get by?
Mumbling along....

~~~~~~~~~~~~~~~~~~~~

Vengeance

Tel me if the sun will shine,
Shall we dine on the blood
Of the devoured
And drink the blood,
From their skulls?
I want to take the bones
Of a child
To beat upon the drums of war
And make my
Vengeance whole...
~~~~~~~~~~~~~~~~~~~~

Collected

I collected words in a book, on paper all around...
Lindum Scribes and distant vibes of drums,
Words from afar and the blue azure of a lure to a sea...
I can bet on England, can't remember a name,
Go down on the golden ship, talk to crazy Susan,
Ask myself is published, "Published?"
It was a little racy for the mothers union,
A divorce anniversary,
A queue of men with pizza and chocolate...
I was gone for a month,
I was showing her my knees,
The kids all look daft,
All grown up, too young to reason...
To start of muddled, to collect
And be collected
To submit these words,
To find time, to the selection process...
The pants are mine,
A rejection slip is gone,
Food for thought and the tiger shark
Another white lie
Say nasty things in writing
And make hay for the day,
Take the collected words
Throw them onto paper,
Don't ask me where it came from,
Why that person is here again?
I just realised, the musical instrument,
The collected legs on glasses
The words,
They make this poem...

Lines...

Age is nothing,
Is this the start of something?

A bridge on glasses,
Spectacles of light
The optical instruments
That helps me see...

A poem about a mirror
That does not reflect
It only sees you as
You see it...

Poppies and Granddad,
War and love...

A love triangle
A forward lady...

The bully forgets,
But never regrets...

A buzzard
Soaring above
The hilltop hamlet...

Time on the train
Past my house again...

Stabbed by the kiss of death,
Held by the lover's words...

A whole spectrum of pomes
And just some lines...

Thank you

Thank you for buying, borrowing or reading this book. If you listened to it, then well I must have done something right along the way...

We learn, we hope from the past. We try to stay clear of confusion and hope that we all get along, only sometimes this is not the case!

If we just smile once in awhile then we can all make the world that little bit less confused, scary and full of hurt, we can instead be human and get along just fine...

Thank you....

Take care and all the best, to those that survived the pandemic of 2019 onwards and to those that did not, we should recall the long and the short and the tall of it all and take this opportunity to make life better for us all, for now and the for tomorrow...

All the best

Ed Chandler